To Daddy

From Frederick

& Dorothy - Rae

Happy Father's Day
2022!

We love you so much ♡

MR. MEN   **LITTLE MISS**

MR. MEN™ LITTLE MISS™ © THOIP (a SANRIO company)

Mr. Men Little Miss My Daddy © 2017 THOIP (a SANRIO company)
Printed and published under license from Penguin Random House LLC
This edition published in 2020 in Great Britain by Farshore
An imprint of HarperCollins*Publishers*
1 London Bridge Street, London SE1 9GF
www.farshore.co.uk

HarperCollins*Publishers*
1st Floor, Watermarque Building, Ringsend Road
Dublin 4, Ireland

ISBN 978 1 4052 9781 3
Printed in the UK
003

MIX
Paper from
responsible sources
FSC™ C007454

FSC
www.fsc.org

MY DADDY

by Roger Hargreaves

and me

My daddy is full of fun from the moment he wakes up.

He is as silly as Mr Funny
and can pull the best faces.

My daddy can do the most impossible things.

And sometimes he can even make my dreams come true.

My daddy is as tall as Mr Tall.

And as strong as Mr Strong.

He is the fastest thing on two legs.

And he can eat the most enormous
plates of food.

My daddy is very clever and knows lots of things.

But he can't always
do everything
he tries.

He reads stories in the loudest, funniest voices.

And I can even hear him
when he's sleeping.

My daddy can sometimes be a bit grumpy, just like me.

But he's always there to help me when I'm tired.

He has a style all of his own.

And sometimes likes things to be just so.

But my daddy is so much fun
and can make anyone smile.

Especially when he tells
his silly jokes.

We do the coolest
things together.

But he also likes a bit of quiet time.

My daddy is full of mischief.

And you have
to watch out
for his tickles.

Life with daddy is one big adventure.

I think he might have even met Father Christmas.

When I'm happy, it makes him happy too.

My daddy is the best daddy
in the whole world.

I love my daddy
and he loves me.

MY DADDY

My daddy is most like **MR.** STRONG

I love it when my daddy reads DIG, DIG, DIG & Goodnight Moon to me.

My daddy makes me laugh when he gets the words wrong on songs & we play fight together

He always knows when I need a cuddle

My daddy is very silly because *he gets the names wrong on Peppa Pig*

My daddy is lots of fun and likes *Mummy*

Our favourite thing to do together is *laugh*

I know he loves me when *we do family cuddles*

My daddy's tickles are the best because *he knows what makes me laugh the most*

This is a picture
of my daddy:

by ....

aged ....